MOTT'S™
A Is for Apple
and all things that grow!

By Megan E. Bryant and Monique Z. Stephens
Illustrated by Liz Conrad

Grosset & Dunlap • New York

A is for apple

and all things that grow.

B is for beans
lined up in a row.

C is for cherries that hang from the trees.

D is for dandelions
that dance on the breeze.

E is for eggplant,

the biggest I've seen.

F is for fiddleheads,

so curly and green.

G is for
green apples

(apples aren't just red!).

H is for honeydew,

as big as your head!

I is for ivy

that climbs up the wall.

J is for Juneberries,
plump, sweet, and small.

Juneberry
JAM

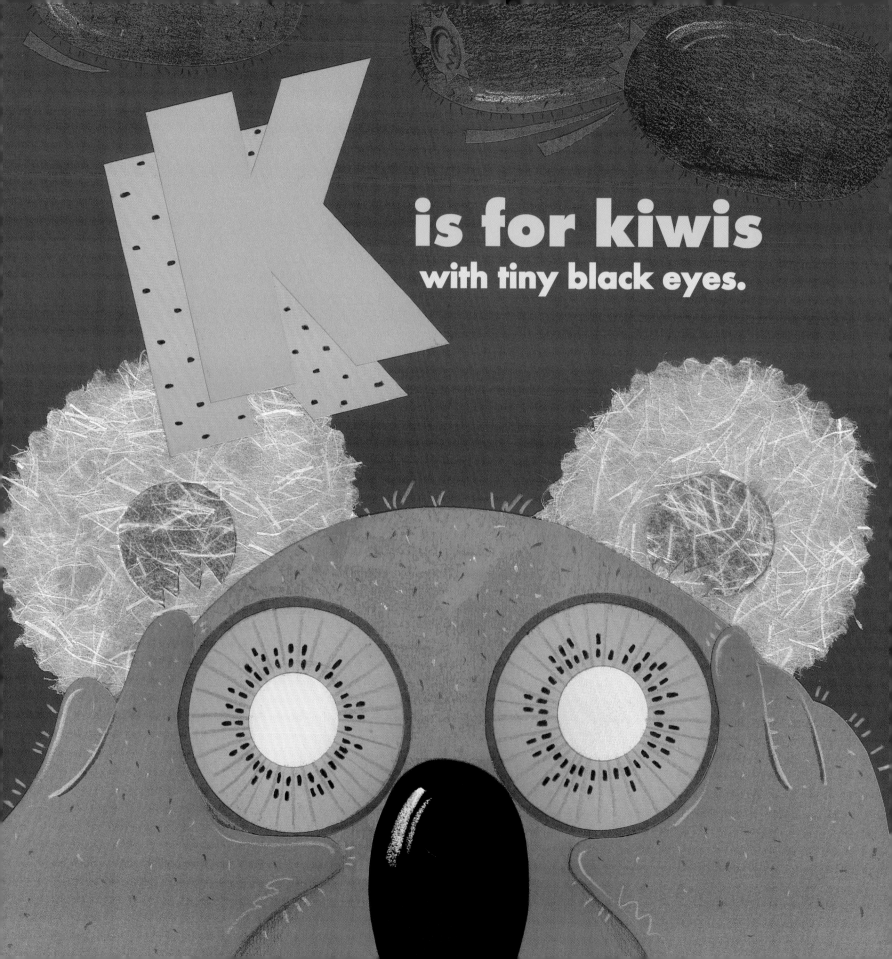

L is for lemons,

a sour surprise.

is for mangoes
made ripe by the sun.

O is for oranges

that drip down your chin.

P is for peaches

with soft, fuzzy skin.

R **is for raisins**

(they're grapes at the start!).

T is for tomato, a fruit that's not sweet.

U is for ugly fruit—

how wrinkly it looks!

V is for violets

that grow by a brook.

W

is for watermelons
that cover the ground.

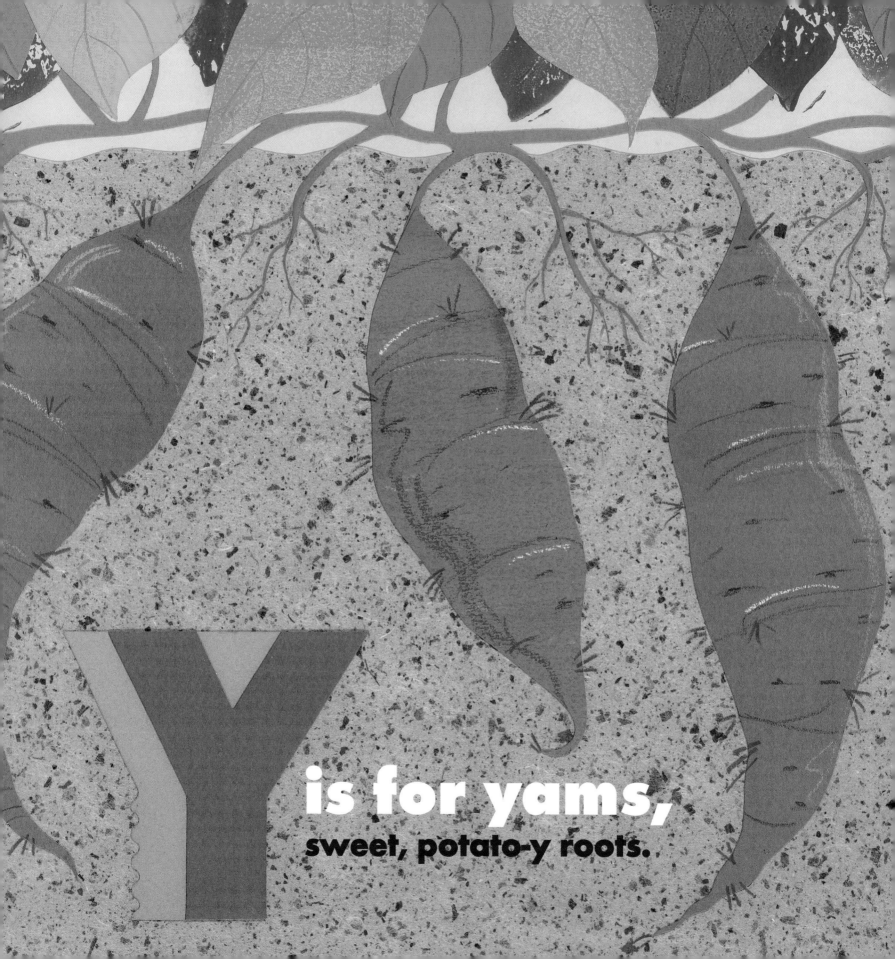

Y is for yams,
sweet, potato-y roots.

Z is for zucchinis,

squash wearing green suits!

Up in trees, on the vine,
or growing underground,

**from apples to zucchinis
ABCs are all around!**

A There are 7,500 different kinds of apples grown in the world. On average, each American eats more than 45 pounds of apples every year!

B Beans have the most protein of any vegetable. Protein is important for strong bones and muscle

C There are two types of cherries: sweet and sour. Sweet cherries are delicious eaten just as they are. Sour cherries are good for using in desserts—especially cherry pie!

D Some people think dandelions are an annoying weed, but they are actually yummy and good f you, too! You can eat the leaves and flowers in a green salad or make tea from the roots. But make sure the dandelions haven't been treated with pesticides or chemicals.

E Eggplants can be black, white, purple, or lavender. Some eggplants are even striped!

F Fiddleheads are the tightly curled leaves of the ostrich fern. Boil them for ten minutes for a quick and delicious vegetable treat.

G Red apples are very popular, but don't forget about great-tasting green apples like Granny Smiths, or even yellow apples like Golden Delicious. (Yep, apples *really* do have great names like these!)

H Honeydew melons have very smooth skin and juicy, pale green flesh. Eat chilled slices for a healthy snack or include them in a yummy fruit smoothie!

I Ivy is a pretty evergreen plant that likes to climb anything it can find—houses, fences, rocks, and even trees! Poison ivy isn't actually a form of ivy at all, but it can cause an itchy red rash—so be careful not to touch it!

J Juneberries are very similar to blueberries. Some people call them saskatoons!

K Kiwis taste tangy-sweet and contain lots of vitamin C. They're also quick and easy to eat: slice them in half and scoop out the fruit with a spoon, or eat them whole, skin and all! (Just be sure t rinse and dry well before eating.)

L Lemons and lemon juice are used in lots of different recipes, including lemonade. Lemons are als used in perfume and even some medicines!

M Mangoes are the most popular fresh fruit in the entire world.

N Everyone loves nuts, and not just people. Squirrels, birds, and other animals also think nuts are a great snack!

O The world's most popular orange to eat is the navel orange. It's called that because the bottom of this fruit looks like a belly button!

P The peach is a member of the rose family, which may help explain its delicious fragrance when it's ripe!

Q A quince looks like a golden apple, but this fruit is tart, not sweet.

R Did you know that raisins start out as regular everyday grapes? The grapes are dried out in the sun, and the dried grapes are called raisins.

S Sunflowers have nutty-tasting seeds that are good to eat. You can eat them raw or toasted.

T Many people think the tomato is a vegetable, but it's not. It's a fruit!

U This unusual looking fruit is a cross between a grapefruit and a tangerine. Its official name is "tangelo," but it's also called ugly fruit because of its wrinkly, weird-looking peel. It may look weird, but it has a sweet, tangy flavor that tastes really good!

V Violets smell great and are pretty to look at, but they're also good to eat! Their blossoms and leaves have lots of vitamin C, and bakers like to use them to decorate fancy cakes.

W Watermelons have the perfect name, because they are about 92% water!

X Christmas melon, also known as Santa Claus melon, gets its name because it keeps for such a long time. If you store an uncut Christmas melon, you can still eat it several months later! (You may be thinking, "Hey! Christmas doesn't start with X!" No, but "X-mas" does, and "X-mas" is short for Christmas!)

Y People often get yams and sweet potatoes confused, but they are not the same thing. In fact, if you ever meet a true yam, you'll see it's not very similar in appearance to a sweet potato at all. Yams can grow up to seven feet in length and weigh up to 150 pounds!

Z Zucchinis are a type of squash. The striped dark green kind is the best known zucchini, but just like squash, zucchini can also be yellow!

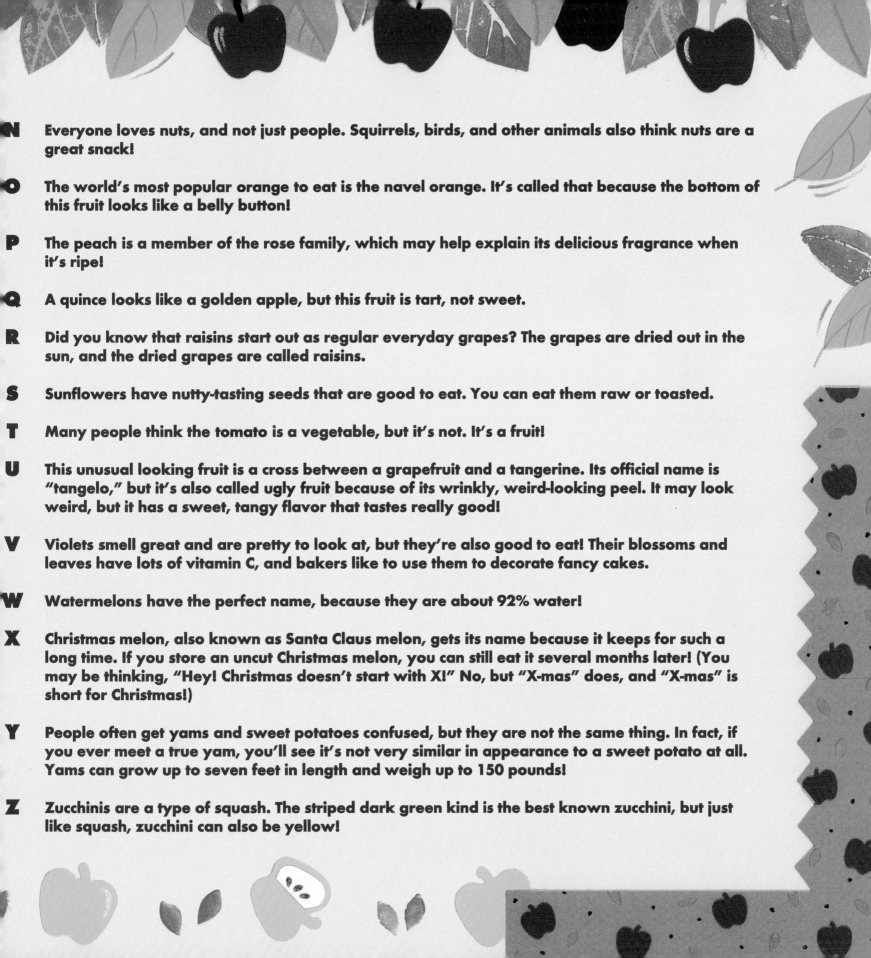

The letters Y and Z have been brought to you by
Olivier Rhee. Thanks.—M.Z.S.

For Judy, with love.—M.E.B.

To Caitlin and Lauren, who have taught me the ABC's of life.—L.C.

0-448-42865-2   A B C D E F G H I J